Usborne
Sparkly Fairy Ponies Sticker Book

Illustrated by Katie Wood

Words by Holly Bathie
Designed by Yasmin Faulkner

You'll find all the sparkly stickers, followed by even more stickers, at the back of the book.

Palaces in the sky

A storm is coming, and Cloud warns the other fairy ponies to find shelter in her palace. Stick them all on here.

In the crystal cave

Deep in the enchanted cave, beautiful crystals glimmer. Add more to the scene, along with curious fairy ponies.

Among the secret ruins

As sunlight shines through the old palace walls, Bolt has spotted Bow hiding behind a column. Stick on the other ponies coming to play.

Dancing at sunset

By the glow of the setting sun, the fairy ponies sparkle and shine as they prance and skip. Stick on Raine and Bolt dancing together.

By the starlit pool

Stars come out one by one, twinkling above the magical pool. Stick on the fairy ponies relaxing in the moonlight.

In the moonlit forest

Stick on tired fairy ponies dreaming of their day, as Lunar sings them to sleep.

Down rainbow lane pages 6–7

In the crystal cave pages 8–9

Down rainbow lane pages 6–7

In the crystal cave pages 8–9

Among the secret ruins pages 10–11

Dancing at sunset pages 12–13